Warbling Winnie

LAURA OWEN & KORKY PAUL

OXFORD

Helping your child to read

Before they start

* Talk about the back cover blurb. Ask your child why it might be a problem if Winnie's voice is considered a bit too "strong".
* Look at the cover picture. Does it give any clues about what might happen in the stories?

During reading

* Let your child read at their own pace, either silently or out loud.
* If necessary, help them to work out words they don't know by saying each sound out loud and then blending the sounds to say the word, e.g. *c-o-n-d-u-c-t-o-r, conductor*.
* Encourage your child to keep checking that the text makes sense and they understand what they are reading. Remind them to reread to check the meaning if they're not sure.
* Give them lots of praise for good reading!

After reading

* Look at page 48 for some fun activities.

Contents

OXFORD
UNIVERSITY PRESS

Great Clarendon Street, Oxford OX2 6DP
Oxford University Press is a department of the University of Oxford.
It furthers the University's objective of excellence in research, scholarship,
and education by publishing worldwide. Oxford is a registered trade mark
of Oxford University Press in the UK and in certain other countries

"Winnie's One-Witch Band" was first published in *Winnie Says Cheese* 2009
"Winnie's Mouse Organ" was first published in *Winnie's Takes the Plunge* 2011
This edition published 2019

The moral rights of the author/illustrator have been asserted

Database right Oxford University Press (maker)

British Library Cataloguing in Publication Data

Data available

ISBN: 978 0 19 276919 0

Winnie's One-Witch Band

⭐ Chapter ⭐ One

Winnie was just pegging out her washing when she heard music coming from the village. She stopped still and listened.

"What is that noise?" Winnie asked Wilbur. "It sounds the way my tummy sounds when I've drunk fizzy-poppy pond-water squash through a straw," she said. "Let's go and find out where it's coming from!"

So Winnie and Wilbur went down into the village. They soon found out that the sound was coming from the library.

"All those people are singing!" said Winnie, as she peeped through the window.

"La, la, la, laaa," warbled the ladies' high-up voices.

"Bom, boom-boom, bom," sang the low-down men's voices.

"Tra-liddle, tra-loddle," they all sang together. "Tra . . ."

They shrieked when they suddenly saw
Winnie's and Wilbur's faces squashed
against the window. "AHHHH!"

"Why have they stopped singing?" asked
Winnie. She soon found out why.

9

The man in charge of the choir was called the conductor. He came to the library door. "Go away!" he said. "You're frightening my choir. We are trying to get ready for a concert."

"What concert?" asked Winnie.

"It's a charity concert for the library," said the conductor. "To raise money to buy more books."

"And who's in the choir?" asked Winnie.

"Anybody who wants to sing," said the conductor.

"Oooh, goody-goody!" said Winnie, pushing her way into the library. "Where do I stand?"

"Well," said the conductor, looking worried. "What kind of voice do you have?"

"A good loud one!" said Winnie.

"No, no," said the conductor, looking even more worried. "What I meant was, do you have a low voice or a high voice?"

11

"Oh, I can go up and down like a kangaroo in a lift!" said Winnie.

"Perhaps I'd better try you out," said the conductor wearily. He sat down at a piano and played. **Plink-plonk-plink-plonk-plink-plonk-plink**. "Now, sing that back to me, please," he told Winnie.

⭐ Chapter ⭐ Two

Winnie opened her mouth and sang.

"**Croak-moan-honk-screechety-croak!**"

Wilbur had his paws over his ears. The choir groaned. The conductor had gone pale. "Er . . ." he said. "I don't think we can use you in our choir, Winnie."

"Why not?" asked Winnie. "Wasn't I loud enough? I can go louder. Listen!"

"Croak-moan-honk-
screechety-croak!"

Books fell from the shelves all around.
The flowers wilted in their vases. Mice ran
for their holes. Bookworms buried themselves
deep into the thickest books they could find.
And the choir all fainted. **Thunk! Thunk!**

"Er . . . no," said the conductor. "I'm afraid that really wasn't good enough."

"Oh," said Winnie. "So you don't want me?"

The conductor shook his head.

There was silence for a moment, then . . .

"Oooh, but I've got a good idea!" said Winnie. "My cat Wilbur has a lovely voice. Why don't you listen to him?"

"Must I?" said the conductor.

"Go on, Wilbur!" said Winnie. "There's absolutely no need to be shy. Everyone wants to hear you sing."

The choir waited nervously. Wilbur meeow-giggled.

Then he sat up straight and opened his mouth. Everyone in the choir covered their ears.

But Wilbur's singing was beautiful.

"Meeow! Mew-mew-mew, meeow-wow!"

As Wilbur sang, the choir took their hands away from their ears and joined in.

"Oh," said the conductor, joyfully. "Oh, Wilbur, that was *wonderful*!" Then he frowned. "But it might look odd if we have a cat in our choir."

"Oh! I know what we can do!" said
Winnie, jumping around in excitement. "If
I wear a long skirt, then Wilbur can hide
under it and sing. I'll just open and close my
mouth and everybody will think it's me who
is singing. It'll look quite normal! I'll show
you. Sing again, please, Wilbur!"

Wilbur sang, "Meeeeeeow! Mew-mew-mew, meeow-wow!"

Winnie silently opened and closed her mouth and waggled her eyebrows. She waved her hands around, knocking the last few books off the shelves. **Thump-thumpety-thump.**

"Good, wasn't it?" said Winnie, when they'd finally got to the end of the song. "Shall I go and find a long skirt?"

"Er . . . no," said the conductor. "I have a better plan! Wilbur can do a solo – *all by himself*. He can perform *with* the choir without being part *of* the choir. Would you like that, Wilbur? Do you have your own bow tie?"

Giggle, went Wilbur. "Meeow." He pretended to be embarrassed.

"Show-off!" said Winnie.

The conductor pointed his baton at Winnie. "You had better leave!"

So Winnie went, stamping her feet crossly like a drum. **Stomp. Stomp.**

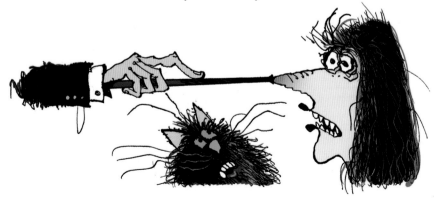

⭐ Chapter ⭐
Three

Winnie went home and cooked herself some tea. **Crash! Bang! Clang!** went the pots and pans. She took her tea out into the garden.

Tweet-tweet went a little bird, like a flute. **Hoot** went an owl, like an organ.

Winnie stopped eating and listened.

Croak-croak-belch went a toad. It sounded like no musical instrument that had ever been invented.

"That has given me a brill-a-rama-roodle idea!" said Winnie suddenly.

She waved her wand. "**Abracadabra!**"

In an instant, Winnie was outside the library, covered in things that made different sounds. She had hooting owls on her shoulders and head. She had a toad in her pocket which croaked when she touched it. She had a rat in another pocket, and when she jiggled its tail, it made a squeal. She had saucepan-lid cymbals strapped on to her knees, and clackety clogs on her feet.

"I'm a one-witch band!" she said. Her wand conducted the music, all on its own.

Crash-clang-croak-squeak, hoot-hoot-hoot-hoot. Ping!

That last ping wasn't really part of the music. It was the elastic snapping on Winnie's knickers!

Inside the library, Wilbur and the choir were singing in the concert.

"Meeeoww!" sang Wilbur.

Winnie played her one-witch band outside the library. **Tra-la-la-la-la, boom-boom-boom!** Lots of people came to listen. They tapped their toes along to the beat. After the choir's concert finished, Wilbur came outside and joined Winnie.

She waved her wand. "**Abracadabra!**"

Instantly, Wilbur had clogs on his paws. He tap-danced to Winnie's band. He held out her hat and collected lots more money for the library. And everybody danced and clapped to Winnie and Wilbur's witch-cat band!

Clank-crash-croak, tappety-tap-parp-whoops!

As they walked home in the moonlight, Winnie said to Wilbur, "When you think about it, life is always better with music."

"Meeow," agreed Wilbur happily.

Winnie's Mouse Organ

✴ Chapter ✴ One

Pong! Phew!

Winnie and Wilbur were flying along with pegs on their noses. They had lots of green, hairy, mouldy cheese in their basket.

"This smelly cheese will get those noisy mice out of their holes," said Winnie. "We'll put the cheese in the mousetrap so that we can catch those mice and get rid of them! Then we'll be able to sleep. We won't have to listen to them **squeakle-squeaking** all night!"

Winnie and Wilbur landed outside the school. There was a big poster on the wall.

"Oooh, look at that, Wilbur!" said Winnie. "What is that shiny snail-shaped thing on the poster? There's a great big nappy pin thing there, too. I wonder what it is?"

Mrs Parmar came out of the school.

Sniff! "What's that awful smell?"
she asked.

"Just cheese," said Winnie. "Do you want
to try some?"

"No, thank you!" said Mrs Parmar. "Ah!
I see that you're looking at our poster. We
want the children to learn all about music."

"Oooh!" said Winnie. "That sounds
brill-a-rama-roodles! I'd love to play one of
those funny things!"

"Can you play an instrument?" asked Mrs Parmar. "If so, you'd be welcome at school this afternoon. We haven't been able to find a musician to come and play for us."

"Oooh, yes, Mrs Parmar!" said Winnie. "I'll show the children how to make lovely music!"

"Meeow!" Wilbur covered his eyes with his paws.

"Which instrument do you play?" asked
Mrs Parmar.

"Oh," said Winnie. "It's . . . er . . . um.
Well, you'll just have to wait and see, Mrs
Parmar. But I'll be along later with my
instrument, don't you worry!"

"Good!" said Mrs Parmar. "I'll tell the
head teacher right away!"

"Wow-zow!" said Winnie, as they flew home. "Oooh, brill-a-rama-roodles! I'm going to be a musician!"

"Meeow?" asked Wilbur.

"Do you want to know how?" said Winnie. "Easy-peasy-turnip-squeezy! I just need to find the perfect instrument and then I'll play it."

She had forgotten all about the mice.

★ Chapter Two ★

Winnie hurried home. As soon as she got inside, she waved her wand. "**Abracadabra!**"

Instantly, there was something that looked like a hairy beast with spikes.

"**Hiss!**" went Wilbur.

"It's a set of bagpipes!" said Winnie. "Listen!" Winnie blew down one of the pipes, and the hairy balloony bag got bigger and bigger.

Then a terrible wailing noise came from the pipes.

"**Hiss!**" Wilbur pounced on the bag.

"You've squashed it!" said Winnie. "What did you do that for? I'll have to try another instrument now." Winnie held her wand up to her mouth. "**Abracadabra!**"

In an instant, Winnie had a shiny trumpet in her hands. "Lovely! I'll do a fanfare!" she said. "Watch this, Wilbur!"

Winnie blew.

No noise came out. Wilbur smiled.

Winnie scowled and blew a raspberry down the trumpet. **Paaarp!**

Wilbur pulled a cushion over his head.

PAAAARP! went Winnie.

"Meeow!" wailed Wilbur.

"Oh, musical maggots, Wilbur! Perhaps I should try something quieter. Perhaps a stringy thingy instrument." Winnie waved her wand like a bow. "**Abracadabra!**"

At once Winnie had a violin. She lifted it up and tucked it under her chin. With her other hand, she began to move the long, thin bow over the strings.

Screeeeech.

"Mee-ow-ow-ow!" screeched Wilbur, even louder. He put his paws over his ears to shut out the awful noise.

"You'll have to go outside, Wilbur!" said Winnie. "I can't learn an instrument with you screeching! Out you go and leave me to practise my music!"

Winnie threw Wilbur out. **Slam!** She shut the door on him.

Suddenly, Winnie heard another, much quieter sound in the room.

"**Squeak-tee-hee!**" It was the sound of mice laughing. The mice wanted to eat the cheese they could smell in Winnie's basket. Now that Wilbur had gone they dared to come out. They weren't frightened of Winnie. Now was their chance!

"**Squeak! Squeak! Sniff-sniff! Scuttle-scuttle!**"

⭐ Chapter ⭐ Three

The mice came out from every corner of the house.

"Go away!" said Winnie as one scuttled over her foot. "Get off!"

"**Squeak!**" went the mouse.

"Oh!" said Winnie. "That was a nice little sound." She gently poked another mouse with her wand.

"**Squeak!**"

"What a lovely low squeak!" she said. "Hmm. I've just had a really *mice* idea!"

Winnie tiptoed to the door and quietly opened it. **Creeeeak!** "Wilbur!" she whispered. "Come back inside and catch some mice for me, but don't hurt them!"

In came Wilbur. He got eight different-sized mice, and put them in a box.

"Right," said Winnie. "Time to go off to the school!"

In the school hall all the children sat
quietly. When they saw the box Winnie
was carrying, they all put their hands in
the air.

"What kind of an instrument is it?"
asked the girl in the front row.

"It's a mouse organ!" said Winnie. "Shall
I show you?"

"Yes, please!" shouted all the children.

So Winnie opened the box. She tipped out the mice. They looked a bit shy. Winnie put them in size order, then she gave one a gentle prod with her finger.

"**Squeak!**" went the mouse.

Giggle! went the children.

Winnie poked another. "**Squeak!**" And another. "**Squeak!**"

"Um . . . is that it?" asked Mrs Parmar.
"Just mice squeaking?"

"Er . . ." said Winnie. Wilbur gave
Winnie her wand.

"Oh, no!" said Mrs Parmar, holding up
a hand. "As I've told you before, Winnie,
absolutely no magic in front of the children!"

"I was just going to use this to conduct the
mice," said Winnie.

"Oh, very well, then," said Mrs Parmar.

Winnie raised her wand. She pretended
to cough but she was actually cough-
whispering, "**Abracadabra!**"

43

And instantly . . .

"We are eight little mice,

Squeak-squeak!

And we sound very nice.

Squeak-squeak!

44

We like to sing this song.

Squeak-squeak!

It isn't very long.

Squeak-squeak!

If you will sing it too,

Squeak-squeak!

We'd love to sing with you.

Squeak-squeak!"

The children laughed and clapped, and they started singing and squeaking along, too. The teachers were delighted.

"Phew!" said Winnie to Wilbur as they left the school. "Nobody noticed the magic, did they?"

Back home, they opened up the box of mice. It seemed a shame to get rid of them now. Winnie and Wilbur both felt quite fond of them.

"Shall we all share some cheese?" said Winnie. "I think there's plenty for everyone."

"Meeow," nodded Wilbur.

"**Squeeeeeak!**" said the mice.

So they all had a pongy cheese party before bed.

"Sweet cheesy dreams, everyone!" yawned Winnie. But the pongy, smelly cheese in their tummies kept them awake all night long!

After reading activities

Quick quiz

See how fast you can answer these
questions! Look back at the stories if
you can't remember.

1) In "Winnie's One-Witch Band", what is
   the concert going to raise money for?
2) In "Winnie's One-Witch Band", why
   does Winnie end up with owls on her
   head and shoulders?
3) In "Winnie's Mouse Organ", what does
   Winnie plan to do with the smelly cheese
   at the start of the story?

1) new books for the library; 2) they are part of her one-witch band;
3) use it to trap the mice

Try this!

★ Make your own one-person band!
   See what noises you can make by
   tapping or shaking things like saucepans,
   plastic pots and packets of rice. Be careful
   not to break anything, though!